The Monkey and the Fishermen

and
The Ass in the Pond

by Val Biro

AWARD PUBLICATIONS LIMITED

Once there was a monkey who lived in the trees.

Once there was a monkey who lived in the trees. Most monkeys do, because they like swinging from branch to branch. This monkey had swung his way through every tree in the jungle.

He liked palm trees best, because of the coconuts.

But he liked the palm trees best, because of the coconuts. He would catch them as they fell, then throw them up and catch them until they fell on the ground and burst. That was the best part because then he could drink the delicious milk and eat the juicy white nut.

One day he looked into the river below.

One day he looked into the river below the tree. He saw the fish swimming about and poking their noses into the air. He thought it would be nice to have some fish for supper.

"I wish I could catch some fish," he said, "but I don't know how."

"I wish I could catch some fish," he said, "but I don't know how. They don't fall off trees like coconuts do."

Just then two fishermen came along, carrying a big net between them.

Just then two fishermen came along the riverbank. They were carrying a big net between them.

"Now, *that* is interesting. I wonder what they're going to do with a net?" thought the monkey.

The monkey watched carefully to see what would happen next.

"Perhaps it's for playing a game, like football or tennis?" The monkey watched carefully to see what would happen next.

The fishermen stretched the net from one side of the river to the other.

One of them crossed the river. Then the fishermen stretched the net from one side of the river to the other, and let it drop into the water.

When the monkey saw this he realised it wasn't a game after all. The net was for catching the fish. What a good idea!

"We should catch lots of fish," they said, and went off to wait in a shady spot.

The fisherman who had crossed the river came back to his friend.

"We should catch lots of fish," they said, and went off to wait in a shady spot round the bend of the river.

At last the monkey knew about fishing. "I shall try it for myself," he said, jumping down from the tree.

At last the monkey knew about fishing.

"I shall try it for myself," he said, jumping down from the tree. "Why didn't I think of it before. All I need is a net, and then I shall have all the fish I want for my supper!" And off he went to find a net.

Soon he found an old net and dragged it down to the river. It was very heavy but he didn't mind.

He knew of an old hut nearby and ran to see what he could find there. Soon he found an old net and dragged it down to the river. It was very heavy but he didn't mind as he was too excited about fishing and a fishy dinner.

He tried to do the same as the
fishermen had done.

When he got back to his tree, he tried to do the same
as the fishermen had done. He tied one end of the net to
a large branch, then jumped into the water with the net.

But he got
so tangled up
that he nearly
drowned.

Poor monkey! He couldn't swim. The net wrapped
itself round his arms and legs and he struggled to get
free, but he got so tangled up that he nearly drowned.

Just then the fishermen came back.

Just then the fishermen came back. "Look!" said one of them. "There is a big furry fish caught in the net! Did you ever see one like it?"

They laughed to see the silly monkey,
but they pulled him out of the river.

They laughed to see the silly monkey, but they pulled him out of the river.

"Just remember," said one of them to the monkey, "there's more to catching fish than you think. You must learn about it first, before you try."

Then the fishermen walked off to see to their own net.

The monkey ran back to his tree.
"I am no good at catching fish," he
said. "I will just catch the coconuts!"

Realising that what the fishermen said was true, the
monkey ran back to his tree.

"I am no good at catching fish," he said. "I will just
catch the coconuts!"

And from that day on, he has never been fishing!

The Ass
in the Pond

An ass had a big load of salt on his back.

An ass had a big load of salt on his back. He was walking home from market behind the farmer who carried nothing but a stick and whistled happily as he walked.

It was difficult to walk because his load was so heavy.

The ass was miserable. He was hot and thirsty and it was difficult to walk because his load was so heavy. But he plodded on, groaning under the weight and slipping and tripping on the rough and dusty road.

He slipped and fell into a pond.
The water washed away
all the salt.

The road was getting rougher and dustier and the ass kept slipping more and more until, suddenly, there was a disaster. He slipped and fell into the pond. *Splash!*

"My salt! My salt!" cried the farmer in alarm, knowing what would happen to his precious salt if it got wet. He tried to pull it out but the water washed away all the salt.

When the ass got out, his load was much lighter.

The ass wasn't worried at all. He enjoyed the nice cool water. When the ass got out his load was much lighter because now the sacks on his back were almost empty.

Now it was the ass who felt cool and light and happy, and the farmer, who had lost all his salt, felt hot and bothered and miserable.

The next day the ass had a big load of sponges on his back.

The next day the ass had a big load of sponges on his back. The farmer had taken him to market again and they were walking back along the same road. It was even hotter and the ass felt most unhappy under his load.

He saw the pond a little way ahead and remembered how much cooler he had felt the day before, after he had fallen in, and how much lighter his load had become.

"I shall try it again," he said to himself.

So he fell into the pond on purpose to make the load lighter.

So he fell into the pond on purpose to make the load
lighter. But this time the farmer was not alarmed at all.
"Oho, my friend! I know what you're up to!" he said
with a grin. "So you thought that the sponges would be
washed away like the salt? Well, climb out and see!"

But the sponges filled up with water and the load was much heavier. Silly ass!

The ass had no idea what the farmer was talking about. He felt much cooler after his soaking, and when he climbed out he expected that his load would be much lighter, too. But the sponges filled up with water and the load was much heavier.

No wonder the farmer had a broad grin on his face, and the ass was scowling miserably. Silly ass!